THE PLANETS

MERCURY
Size: 4,880 km (3,050 miles) in diameter
Average distance from the sun: 57,900,000 km (36,200,000 miles)

VENUS
Size: 12,100 km (7,600 miles) in diameter
Average distance from the sun: 108,200,000 km (67,625,000 miles)

EARTH
Size: 12,756 km (7,973 miles) in diameter
Average distance from the sun:
  149,600,000 km (93,500,000 miles)

THE MOON
Size: 3,476 km (2,173 miles) in diameter
Average distance from Earth:
  384,000 km (240,000 miles)

MARS
Size: 6,794 km (4,246 miles) in diameter
Average distance from the sun: 227,392,000 km (142,120,000 miles)
Mars has two moons, Deimos and Phobos.

THE ASTEROIDS (the small planets)
There are hundreds of small planets in a belt between Mars and Jupiter. The largest is called Ceres.

JUPITER
Size: 143,200 km (89,500 miles) in diameter
Average distance from the sun: 778,300,000 km (486,440,000 miles)
Jupiter has at least seventeen moons.

SATURN
Size: 120,000 km (75,000 miles) in diameter
Average distance from the sun: 1,427,000,000 km (892,000,000 miles)
Saturn has at least twenty-two moons. Saturn's rings are made of small particles covered by ice.

URANUS
Size: 51,800 km (32,400 miles) in diameter
Average distance from the sun: 2,870,000,000 km (1,793,750,000 miles)
Uranus has at least fifteen moons.

NEPTUNE
Size: 49,500 km (30,940 miles) in diameter
Average distance from the sun: 4,497,000,000 km (2,810,625,000 miles)
Neptune has eight moons.

PLUTO
Size: 3,000 km (1,875 miles) in diameter
Average distance from the sun: 5,900,000,000 km (3,687,500,000 miles)
Pluto has one moon, Charon. Until 1999 Pluto will be in an orbit closer to the sun than Neptune, but most of the time it is farther away. It is always referred to as the most distant planet in our solar system.

Thanks to
Stina, Robin, and Tom
and
the Astronomical Society of Östergötland
and
Norrköping's Amateur Astronomical Club

Thanks also to Marie Rådbo in the astronomy department
at Chalmers Technical College/University of Gothenburg,
who checked the text

Rabén & Sjögren Stockholm

Translation copyright © 1992 by Steven T. Murray
All rights reserved
Originally published in Sweden by Rabén & Sjögren
under the title *Resan i rymden,* pictures and text copyright © 1990 by Gunilla Ingves
Library of Congress catalog card number: 91-42416
Printed in Singapore
First edition, 1992

ISBN 91 29 62058 9

R & S Books are distributed in the United States of America by
Farrar, Straus and Giroux, New York;
in the United Kingdom by Ragged Bears, Andover;
in Canada by Vanwell Publishing, St. Catharines;
and in Australia by ERA Publications, Adelaide

Gunilla Ingves

To Pluto and Back

A Voyage in the Milky Way

Translated by Steven T. Murray

Esther

Stina, 10

Tom, 11

Robin, 8

Fluff

R&S
BOOKS

Stockholm   New York   London   Adelaide   Toronto

High up in the big climbing tree there is a blue rocket. Stina, Robin, and Tom built it out of old boards. They're going to outer space in this rocket. Their dog, Esther, and their cat, Fluff, are going along for the ride.

Ad Astrum means "toward the star."

Robin is looking at the Sea of Crises. It is the little dark spot on the far right side of the moon. All the dark spots on the moon are huge plains. Astronauts have landed on some of these plains in their spacecraft. Robin wonders where he and Stina and Tom will land when they reach the moon.

Map of the Moon

Bay of Rainbows

Sea of Rains

Archimedes

Sea of Serenity

Sea of Crises

Copernicus

Tycho

They look at their moon map. Robin wants to go to the Sea of Crises. Stina wants to travel to a place called the Bay of Rainbows. It makes no difference to Tom. They have to draw lots to decide where they'll go. Tom is hiding a rock in one hand. If Robin finds the rock, they'll go to the Sea of Crises. He points at Tom's left hand. Tom opens his hand. There's the rock. Robin draws in the blue rocket next to the Sea of Crises.

They're going to travel to the planets, too. Stina searches for the planet Mars in the sky. The planets look like stars, but they don't twinkle. They shine with a steady glow. Tom's almanac says that Mars can be seen in the constellation of Taurus just now. Stina finds the planet. It's shining very brightly, because it is very close to earth at this time.

It's starting to get cold outside. Stina, Tom, and Robin go inside the rocket. They have to make a map of our solar system. Tom paints the sun in the middle of a big piece of dark-blue paper. Stina wants to draw the planet Mercury. It's the one closest to the sun. She's going to draw it the correct size and at the correct distance from Tom's sun. Stina calculates and measures. Mercury won't fit on the map. Stina draws it as a little tiny dot over by the door. And out in the yard Robin shouts: "This is where Pluto would be. What a giant map! We can't make a map that big."

Instead they just paint the planets in the order they travel around the sun. First Mercury, then Venus, Earth, Mars, the asteroids, Jupiter, Saturn, Uranus, Neptune, and finally Pluto. Tom calculates how long it will take to travel to the moon, the sun, and the planets under rocket power. It will take seventy hours to reach the moon. To reach the planets would take them months, even years. They decide to travel at the speed of light to reach the sun and the planets. That way, it will take only five hours to go all the way to Pluto. But they're going to the moon on rocket power. Otherwise, they'd arrive before they could count to two. Stina draws their route with a red pen.

Robin wants to visit one of the stars in the Big Dipper. But the stars are far, far away. It would take about seventy-eight years, traveling at the speed of light, to reach Merak, one of the stars in the Big Dipper. With normal rocket power it would take a little more than two million years to get there. It's hard to believe that we can see something so far away! It's a good four light-years to the nearest star.

Merak

They spend the whole next day getting ready and packing for the trip. They fill their backpacks with their favorite things and their clothes. They take out their sleeping bags and their space suits. The suits will protect them from bitter cold, burning heat, and the sun's rays, which are dangerous in outer space. They have to take oxygen along to breathe, since there's no air out in space. Esther sees that they're packing. She sits down by the sleeping bags. She wants to be sure they take her along. Mom puts a big basket of food inside the rocket.

14

Early the next morning, when everyone else is asleep, Robin, Tom, and Stina go out to the rocket with all their baggage. It smells good outside, and the grass is damp with morning dew. Their shoes get a little wet. Up in the sky the planet Venus is shining like a bright star. Fluff is the first to climb up to the rocket. They have to help Esther up the ladder.

They have butterflies in their stomachs and their hearts are pounding when they start the engines. The rocket starts to shake. With a jolt it rattles up through the leaves of the tree. The magpies that live in the tree scatter in every direction. They screech in fright.

The rocket climbs higher and higher. It zooms through the clouds and into the upper atmosphere. In ten minutes they're already in the darkness of space. The Earth looks like a gigantic bowl of blueberry soup with dabs of whipped cream on it. The blue is the ocean. The cream is the clouds hovering above the Earth. They fly past a weather satellite. It takes pictures of the weather all over the world.

The Earth grows smaller and smaller. At this point it's so far away that it can't attract the rocket any longer. Tom, Robin, and Stina feel as light as feathers. They are weightless now that they have escaped Earth's gravity. Tom and Robin float down to the galley to get some food. Fluff howls in fright and puffs up her tail when she discovers she can't walk normally. Tom grabs her and calms her down.

Stina and Robin put on their space suits. Esther wants to go outside with them. She barks and barks. They float out onto the balcony through an air lock. All three are wearing safety lines so that they won't fly off into space and disappear. Tom and Fluff stay behind in the rocket. Tom has to change course now and then, because the moon keeps moving in its path around the Earth. Tom turns on the radio so he can hear the news from Earth.

Outside the rocket it is totally silent. Esther is still barking, but they can't hear her anymore. Where there is no air, there can't be any sound. Stina and Robin try to talk in sign language with each other. The sun is shining on the balcony. It's 150 degrees Celsius (300 degrees Fahrenheit). Almost as warm as the oven when they bake sponge cake! It's a good thing that it's always the right temperature inside their space suits.

Stina and Robin jump off the balcony. They move around to the other side of the rocket, which is in shadow. Esther sits on the wing of the rocket and pees. The urine freezes at once to a cloud of ice crystals. Here on the shady side it's −170 degrees Celsius (−270 degrees Fahrenheit)! Stina and Robin look at the Earth. It hangs like a glowing blue ball among the stars.

When they are back on the balcony again, Stina catches sight of a rock that is flying through space. It's a meteorite. It might be a piece of an old comet or asteroid. Stina and Robin watch the meteorite move down toward Earth. When it enters Earth's atmosphere (air), it starts to glow. Down there on Earth it looks like a shooting star.

23

Tom, Robin, and Stina take turns sleeping. They can't stay awake all the way to the moon. Before they fall asleep, Robin and Tom look at the moon. At the Bay of Rainbows it's morning. Over by the Sea of Crises it's afternoon. On the moon the days and nights are very long. One moon day lasts for two weeks, and then it's night for just as long.

After seventy hours they reach the moon. On the day side the sun shines across the plains, mountains, and craters. They fly in over the Sea of Rains. It seems funny that the plains are called seas, because there isn't a drop of water on the moon. But long ago, the scientists thought that the dark spots on the moon were seas. That's why they named them that way. Stina is flying over the crater of Archimedes.

Tom looks at the map of the moon. He explains to Stina where they are. Near the Sea of Tranquillity she makes the rocket descend lower and lower. Robin keeps watching the ground. On the other side of the Sea of Tranquillity, among mountains and craters, lies the Sea of Crises. They're finally here! Esther starts barking when she hears their happy shouts. Esther wants to go out. Out to dig and run around.

With a bump they land silently on the Sea of Crises. Robin, Stina, and Tom hurry out of the rocket, along with Esther and Fluff. When they jump down onto the moon, the soft, dark moondust puffs up around them. They are so light that they bounce along. It feels like walking on a trampoline. The sun shines down from the black sky. It's hot, 150 degrees Celsius (302 degrees Fahrenheit). Robin kicks his soccer ball hard. It . . .

... flies far away. He was never able to kick the ball that far back home on Earth. Suddenly a meteorite falls from the sky. With tremendous force it crashes into the moondust. The meteorite breaks up and the pieces fly in every direction. One of the meteorite pieces lands right at Stina's feet.

They examine the meteorite. It's dark, almost black, with little white spots here and there. Stina takes out her rock book, which has pictures of meteorites. One of them looks like theirs. The book says it is rare and that it probably comes from a comet. Robin stuffs the meteorite into his treasure bag. Now they have to gather more rocks. But where is Esther?

Esther is gone. They don't see her anywhere. Stina tries to call Esther. But she has forgotten that you can't hear any sounds on the moon. It's just as silent here as it is out in space. Tom points at Esther's tracks. They're easy to see. Esther's tracks will be on the moon forever. There will never be a storm here to wipe them away. Robin picks up Fluff. They follow Esther's tracks in the gray moondust.

Far off, behind a big crater, they find Esther. She looks scared. She couldn't sniff her way back along her tracks. Even if Esther had not been wearing her space helmet, she wouldn't have been able to smell anything. There isn't any air on the moon, and there has to be air for there to be any smells. Now Robin, Tom, and Stina are tired. Even though it's daytime, they have to go back to the rocket and sleep. First they fill up the treasure bag with rocks that they find near the crater.

When night falls at the Sea of Crises, they leave the moon. Stina writes in the logbook:

Sept. 7: Night at the Sea of Crises. The Earth shines just like a moon. Robin takes a picture of the Sea of Crises in the earthlight. Tom has filled a whole bucket with moondust. He's going to try to grow things in it when he gets home. Now we're going to fly the rocket at the speed of light toward the sun. But first we'll put on our special goggles. They'll protect us from the bright sunlight!

Stina pushes the button for the speed of light. The arrow on the
speedometer quivers up toward 300,000 kilometers (186,000 miles)
per second. Wow! After half a minute they are far away from the
moon. Now the moon and the Earth are shining no brighter than
stars in the distance.

The rocket zooms toward the sun. The sun grows bigger and
bigger. It shines brighter and brighter.

The light of the sun grows tremendously bright. Finally there is nothing but one huge light shining all around them. The surface of the sun glows and bubbles. It shoots out huge flames. They can't get any closer, because the flames are at least 150,000 kilometers (93,000 miles) long. Robin looks at his watch. It took them eight minutes to fly to the sun at the speed of light. That's just as long as it takes a ray of sunlight to reach Earth. Tom turns the rocket around. He flies . . .

. . . away from the hot sun. They see the brownish-red planet Mercury. It's only a little bigger than the moon, and full of craters and mountains. Mercury is close to the sun. It's terribly hot there. They keep on going toward Venus. Stina and Robin try to see how many times they can play "Twinkle, Twinkle, Little Star" on their flutes before they get there.

When Stina and Robin have played the tune four times, they can see Venus up close. Tom and Stina go out onto the balcony to have a look. Venus looks like a soft ball of clouds. The creamy-white clouds glitter in the bright sunlight. Robin flies them cautiously around Venus. With their binoculars Tom and Stina search for a break in the cloud cover. They want to see what it looks like down on Venus, and where they can land. There is not a cloud-free spot anywhere.

Robin flies into the clouds. It's bright and foggy. The rocket disappears deeper and deeper into the cloud cover. Piercing bolts of lightning rip through the clouds. The lightning comes from every direction. Everything is blindingly bright. They have to shut their eyes. Esther pushes her nose under Stina's arm. Her whole body is quivering with fear. The rocket shakes and the boards creak. Stina, Robin, and Tom move closer to each other.

Finally they are out of the clouds. But the clouds are still hanging above them, thick and heavy with lightning. The thunderstorm rumbles. It's burning hot, almost 500 degrees Celsius (approximately 900 degrees Fahrenheit). Through a reddish light they can see the vast plains and high mountains. Then a gust of wind grabs the rocket. They fly through the hot, heavy air. Suddenly a cliff towers up in front of them. Robin quickly pulls back on the control stick to climb. But the stick can't be budged. It's jammed!

38

All three pull on the stick as hard as they can. It snaps back, and with a roar the rocket zooms up through the clouds. Stina, Robin, and Tom are shaking all over. It feels wonderful to be out in calm, silent space again. After traveling for five minutes they see Earth. They fly slowly for a while, just looking. Back home it's daytime. The weather is sunny; there are no clouds over Sweden. Stina and Robin float out with the tool box. They tighten some screws that loosened during the storm. When they come back inside, Tom sets their course for Mars.

It doesn't take long before they're approaching the rust-red planet and its moons, Deimos and Phobos. The moons look like two dirty potatoes. There are only a few thin white clouds floating over Mars. With his binoculars Robin can see the snowy poles, the volcanoes, the mountains, the craters, the deserts, and the dried-up riverbeds. Tom and Stina look at the map of Mars. They're searching for a place called Valles Marineris. It's somewhere near the equator of Mars. They want to fly there and pick up rocks. But first . . .

... they land at the south pole of Mars. They trudge out through the snow. It feels almost like being home in Sweden on a snowy winter day. But they can't take off their space helmets, because there is nothing but carbon dioxide in the air here, and it's −100 degrees Celsius (−150 degrees Fahrenheit). The sun is shining up in the pink sky. It looks smaller from here than from the Earth. They play for a while in the snow before they climb into the rocket and fly to ...

... Valles Marineris. Stina, Robin, and Tom pick out a whole heap of rocks by the dried-up rivers. They want to know whether there was life here when there was water in the riverbeds. With the magnifying glass they search for fossils or prints of plants and animals in the rocks. They search all day, but they don't find any trace of life at this spot. When the sun goes down and night falls they go to bed and sleep. The next morning after breakfast they start the rocket.

They fly up through the pink atmosphere and out into the darkness toward the asteroid belt. They pass by an asteroid. It looks like a rocky island full of little mountains and craters. Robin is petting Esther and Fluff. Tom takes care of his plants while Stina flies to the biggest of all the planets . . .

. . . Jupiter. On the way in toward Jupiter they pass by the orange moon, Io. Closer to Jupiter, they don't dare fly into the stormy clouds, which are miles deep. Jupiter's gravity is enormous. They would never get out if they flew down there. Before they leave Jupiter and its seventeen moons, they take a look at Jupiter's Great Red Spot. There's always a hurricane there. The spot is huge, bigger than Earth. Now they're hungry. Tom floats down to the galley to get yogurt and sandwiches.

After flying for half an hour they catch sight of Saturn. The planet shines a pale yellow-orange. Icy dust particles and rocks fly in the rings around Saturn, round and round like a carousel. Most of Saturn's twenty-two moons orbit outside the rings.

Tom, Robin, and Stina leave Saturn. They travel farther out into space, past Uranus — the planet with the bluish-green clouds. Several hours later they reach . . .

. . . the planet Neptune. It is large and a shimmering blue. Stina and Robin make a drawing of the planet. They use three different pieces of light-blue chalk to show the shimmer. Tom tells them that it's icy cold outside — —214 degrees Celsius (—353 degrees Fahrenheit). Down below, beneath the clouds, Neptune is covered by ice-slush hundreds of miles deep. Tom flies away from Neptune, past its eight moons. They travel on to the farthest and smallest planet in the solar system.

Lonely, but close to each other, Pluto and its moon, Charon, wander through the cold. The sun looks tiny. It shines from far, far away. It casts a weak glow on the icy planet and its moon. The ice crystals glitter like diamonds in the faint twilight. A comet sweeps past. It looks like a dirty iceberg.

    Robin, Tom, and Stina are tired. Along with Esther and Fluff, they float up to the sleeping cabin. They creep into their sleeping bags and fall asleep. The rocket continues deeper into space.

When they wake up it's completely dark, just like night. They turn on the lamps inside the rocket and float out onto the balcony. The sun is so far away that it doesn't give them light anymore. It shines like a star among the other stars. All stars are suns. What if there are plants, animals, and people on

some other planet near some other sun? Scientists have sent radio messages and listened for sounds from several thousand stars, but they haven't heard anything yet. Stina, Robin, and Tom have made their own radio telescope.

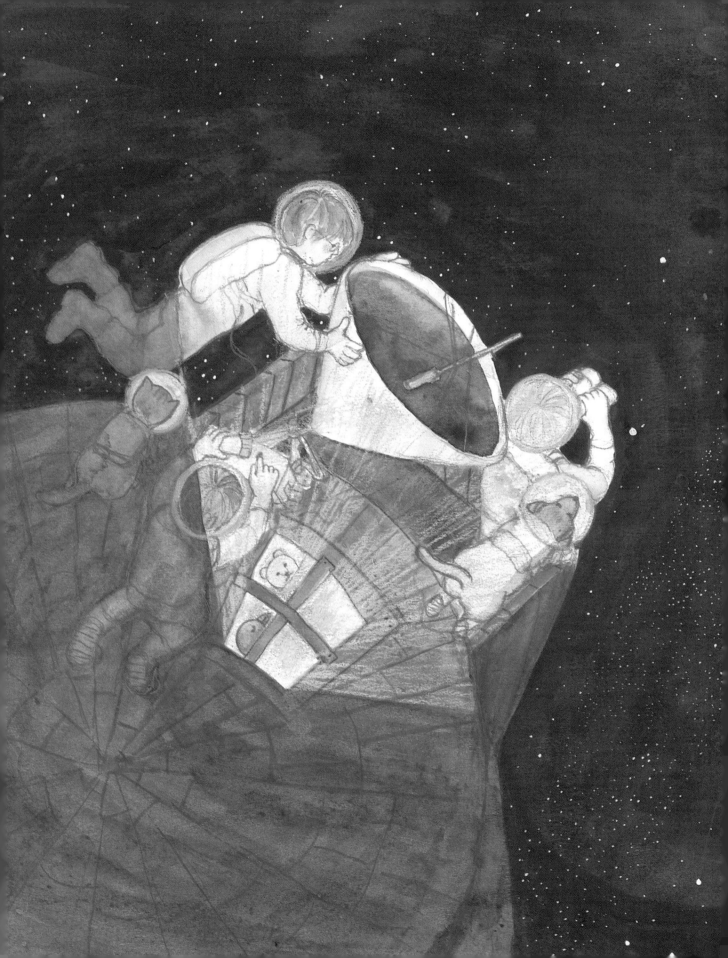

Capella

They fasten it to the roof of the rocket. Robin searches for the star Capella. He finds it in the constellation Auriga, the Charioteer. (The star and Auriga are marked in the picture so you can find them, too.) It's forty-five light-years to Capella. Tom points the radio telescope at Capella. Stina pushes the key in long and short signals (like Morse code). Now it will take forty-five years before the signals are heard at Capella. If they got an answer, that would take another forty-five years. By that time Robin will be 98, Stina 100, and Tom 101 years old.

Tom tells Stina and Robin that there are huge, glowing, colored gas clouds out among the stars. One of the clouds is called the Orion Nebula. New stars are born there from the dust and gases. The cloud looks like a tiny scrap of fog in the sky when we see it from Earth.

The Milky Way Galaxy

Our sun

Now they can't travel any farther out into space. The rocket is powered by solar-energy batteries, and soon they will need new power from the sun's rays.

Tom and Stina look at a picture of our own galaxy, the Milky Way. There are billions of stars. The arrow is pointing to our sun.

Robin looks out the rocket window. Near the constellation Orion, the sun twinkles invitingly at him. Out there somewhere is Earth. Robin wants to go home; it will take only twelve hours, since they are not going to stop anywhere.

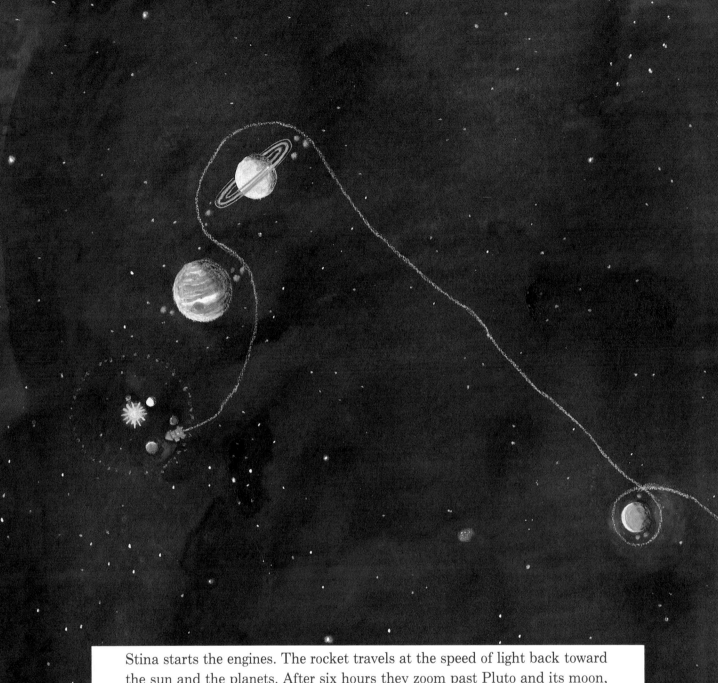

Stina starts the engines. The rocket travels at the speed of light back toward the sun and the planets. After six hours they zoom past Pluto and its moon, Charon.

At Neptune, Robin trades places with Stina at the control stick. When it's time to eat dinner they see Uranus. Robin puts the rocket into an orbit around the planet. While they eat dinner they gaze at Uranus and its fifteen moons.

After dinner Robin sets the course toward Saturn. Then it will be Tom's turn to drive. He flies to Jupiter and farther in past the asteroids. Now they're almost home. After fifteen minutes they catch sight of Mars and its moons, Deimos and Phobos. Four minutes later . . .

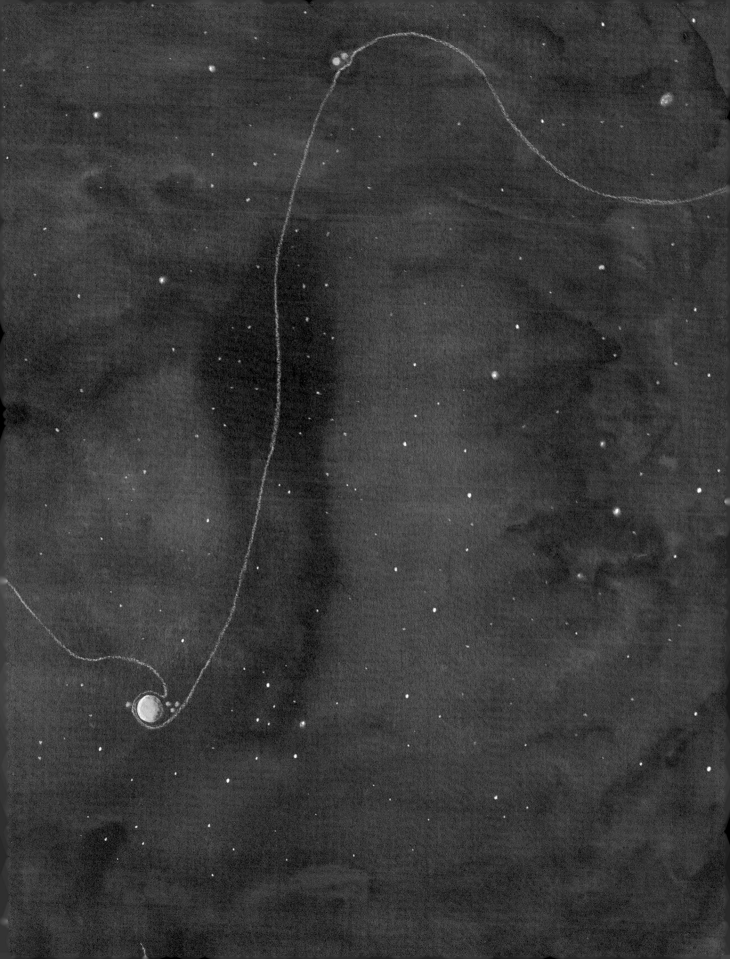

... Tom slows down. He flies at half the speed of light past the moon. Then he slows down even more. They're approaching Earth. Down there under the clouds they glimpse the continents and the blue oceans. It's daytime at home. Tom sees where they're going to land.

Robin and Stina come in from the balcony and put on their seat belts. Earth's gravity starts pulling in the rocket. Tom brakes. He brakes more and more. They're coming closer and closer to Earth.

Slowly they fly into Earth's atmosphere. The sun is shining above the puffy clouds. It feels like flying along over soft cotton balls. Through a crack in the cloud cover they see their house and their climbing tree.

The rocket drops slowly toward the ground, and with a thud it lands in the tree. They hear the magpies screeching. Stina opens the door. Esther dashes out of the rocket and starts barking wildly. Fluff sneaks out behind her, slowly and carefully. She sniffs the air.

Stina, Tom, and Robin stretch, they're so stiff after the journey. The wind ruffles their hair. It has just rained, and they can smell the wet leaves and soil. They look up at the sky. There they see the moon. It's still nighttime at the Sea of Crises.

Stina, Tom, and Robin have completed their trip. But we are always traveling through space. The Earth, our big, shimmering blue spaceship, travels along with the sun and all the other planets around and around in our island of stars, the Milky Way galaxy.

WOULD YOU LIKE TO KNOW MORE?

There are lots of guides for amateur astronomers to choose from if you want to learn how to study the planets and the stars in the sky. One good basic handbook is *A Field Guide to the Stars and Planets* by Jay M. Pasachoff and Donald H. Menzel (Boston: Houghton Mifflin, 1893); you can also ask your local librarian to recommend some books.

Almanacs, which generally come out once a year, usually contain star maps, a map of the moon, and information on when and where you can see the various planets. Usually, they also give the distances to a number of stars, nebulas, and galaxies. Two almanacs that are useful — and easy to find at the library or in a bookstore — are *The Old Farmer's Almanac,* which contains everything from astronomical tables, tides, and eclipses to planting tables and "zodiac secrets," and *The World Almanac,* which gives you "celestial events highlights."

You can also join an amateur astronomy club and study the stars and planets with other people. Many cities have an observatory (that is occasionally open to the public) or a planetarium, which lets you see a representation of the sky.

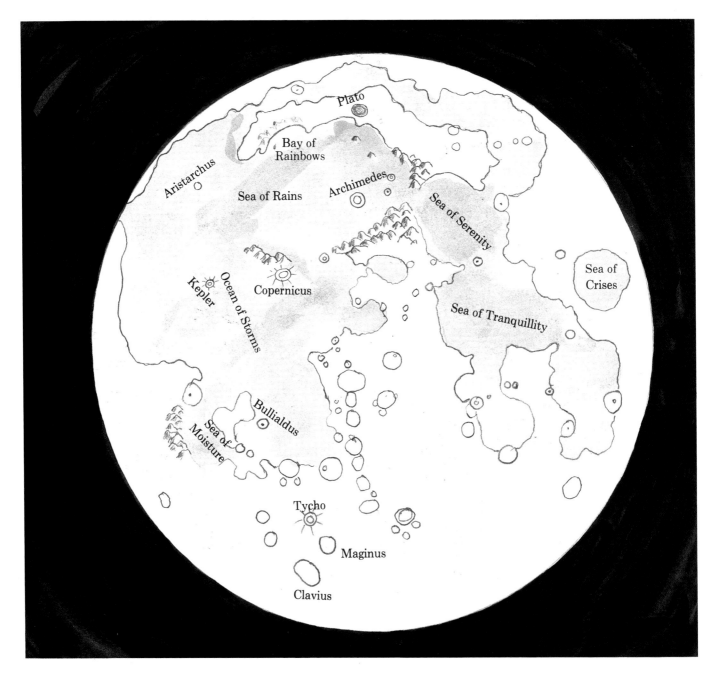

WHEN YOU LOOK AT THE MOON

In many star calendars the phases of the moon are indicated by the following symbols:

◐ half moon, first quarter (waxing)   ○ full moon
◑ half moon, third quarter (waning)   ● new moon

The mountains and craters are easiest to see when they are at the edge of the moon's day and night sides. When Robin and Tom look at the moon through the window of the rocket, it is four days past the first quarter. The bright walls of the crater Aristarchus rise out of the moon's night side. The mountains by the Sea of Moisture arc outward. The big crater of Tycho looks like the navel of an orange. See page 24.

You can see the crater Archimedes, which Stina flies over, when the moon is in the first quarter. The crater walls arc outward toward the black night side. The bottom of Archimedes is dark. It lies in shadow.

When you look at the moon it's a good idea to brace your binoculars against something so they're steady.

HOW TO FIND THE PLANETS

The planets shine strongly and with a steady light. *The World Almanac* lists what time of the year the planets can be seen and what constellations they pass through. The planets aren't really traveling through the stars. It just looks that way from down here on Earth. Star maps tell you where to look for the various constellations. Some constellations are hard to find. It's a good idea to find an easy constellation near the hard one you're looking for.

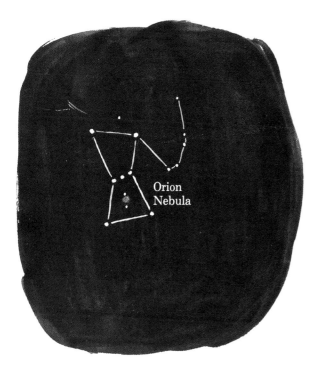

THE ORION NEBULA

This can be seen with binoculars. It looks like a weakly shining patch of fog below the three stars in Orion's belt. The constellation Orion is seen only in the winter and early spring — in Sweden, that is! You'll see it in the southeast, very low in the sky. The later at night you look, the higher up in the sky it will be — and the farther toward the southwest.

THE ANDROMEDA GALAXY

You should be out in the countryside where it's dark when you look at the Andromeda galaxy. To find the galaxy, first find the constellation Cassiopeia. It's easy to recognize — it looks like a W. To the right and below the W lies the constellation Pegasus. From there you follow the three right-hand stars in the constellation Andromeda and stop. Now count three smaller stars up toward Cassiopeia. It's not easy, but there you will find the Andromeda galaxy at last. It looks like a little patch of fog. It feels wonderful to stand there and be able to see something so distant. The galaxy is more than two million light-years away!

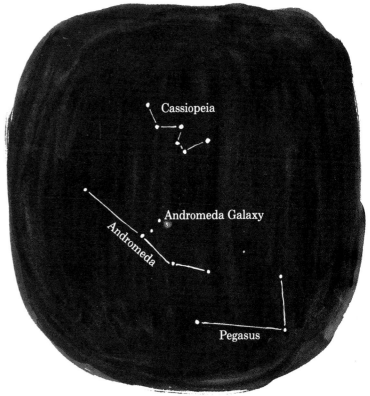

61